FOREVER YOURS

Getting over depression and the Tough Time

Written By: **AMUSAN AISHAT**

Edited By: **Nasir Taofik**

Published By: NASS INNOVATION

ISBN: 9798352376171

DEDICATION

This book is dedicated to my loved ones and my Entire Family.

CONTENTS

Title page
Copyright
Dedication
The Editor
Characters
Prologue

1 ACT ONE

2 ACT TWO

3 ACT THREE

4 ACT FOUR

5 ACT FIVE

6 ACT SIX

7 ACT SEVEN

8 ACT EIGHT

9 ACT NINE

10 ACT TEN

11 ACT ELEVEN

12 ACT TWELVE

13 ACT THIRTEEN

Acknowledgments

About the Author

Untitled

CHARACTERS

Gilbert Katherine (Leonard Lauren's friend).
Mrs. Edna Gilbert (Katherine mother).
Mr. Myles Gilbert (Katherine father).
Daniel king (Katherine fiancée).
Leonard Lauren.
Late Mr. Leonard.
Late Mrs. Leonard.
Dylan (Lauren First younger sister).
Irene (second Lauren younger sister).
Desmond (Leonard family Gateman).
Jacob James (Leonard Lauren fiancée).
Mrs. James (Jacob mother).
Barros James (Jacob elder brother).
Mr. Haley king (Daniel father).
Kate (Daniel king step mother).
Uber Driver.
Hospital Receptionist.
Doctor Teddy.
Nurse 1.
Nurse 2.
Rose (Store Assistant).

PROLOGUE

She exhaled and inhale, the world started to swim in front of her eyes, she found herself on the dead end of a cliff, a greeny tree sheltered her, forming a shallow shadow of a paraplegics as the thought flows, death seems to be a perfect answer for she lost her world and became a limbless nymph that would remain sedentary for the rest of her life, She unwrapped the shaddy rope, her heart thuds.

ACT ONE

Loss
(THE BEGINNING)

(it's the end of first semester for Kathrine and Lauren in the university. Lauren Leonard steps out of her hostel in a wheelchair as the casters rolled roughly on the ramp, holding a thick rope, she heads to the back of the hostel where there is a mango tree, she was going to commit suicide, she wants to hang herself to death all in the name of getting depressed, she had forgotten she's about to commit the worst of sin. Kathrine Gilbert, she is Lauren very good friend, she saw her moving out of the hostel building and she also knew she hasn't been herself since her parent died and she became paraplegic, Lauren hasn't been active in all aspect of life. Katherine decided to trace her and to know what she's up to. From distance Kathrine sight Lauren, she was about to slot the rope in her neck. Katherine picked a race to Stop Lauren.)

Lauren Leonard: (sobs cynically) and what am I even still doing on earth? I have lost my two lovers an on the same day, no one to give me parental word of thought or advice. none to cares for me. My legs are stiffened, Oh lord! I do not deserve this loss, I miss my parent. Not having them around makes me feel depressed, lonely and tiring, I can't even concentrate on my school work (exhale). I don't think I can bear this any longer, I will rather die and be with them than to be lashed by depression. Dylan! Irene! I am so sorry I had to leave you two. The lord will be with you.

Katherine Gilbert: (desisting) No! No!! You can't Lauren, For God sake, why are you doing this? What has come over you? Is this the solution to what has happened? Would this bring your parent back to life? would this bring forth love you yearned or would this replenish your legs? ahn,

Lauren? (She unwrapped the rope around her neck) let's thinks about it once more, ohm.

Lauren Leonard: (she sobs) when I thought about my life, the world seems to have come to an end, all I could say to myself was let's end it here (she holds onto her).

Katherine: sweetie, start it all over and only then could you see that this world is up full of love and peace. Lauren: Are you sure?

Katherine: Of course, would I lie to you? Have faith darling.

Lauren: (misanthropic) faith? In this situation, Katherine you know I lost faith with my parent's demise. I trusted their words of staying with me forever, but they left me.

Katherine: (speaks astringently) They didn't leave because they wanted to, destiny played a chess game on them. Besides, had it been the road wasn't slippery and the oil tank brakes didn't failed while they were driving down the express then the accident might not have happened. It's so unfortunate that you couldn't walk due to shock. You were unconscious for weeks, several seizures in a day, at some point the doctors thought you wouldn't make it. You've come this far sweetie, believe in yourself and in no time, you will get over everything.

Lauren: (relieved) Katherine... (She cries softly)

Katherine: (softly) Sorry, just let go home, your younger ones are worried to death, they have been calling me when they can't reach. What are you even thinking? You don't even think about these little girls. Let's go into this hostel.

Lauren: okay. (She blends and sprinkle water on her face to clear up her tears). Katherine: Good of you girl.

Lauren: Girl?! Katherine: Oh, sorry my lady (she scoff) uhm! (In slam voice) (they both set for Lauren's house) (They arrived at Lauren's house and her younger ones give them a warm embrace).

Dylan and Irene: (Lauren's sisters) (excited) you are back sister Lauren, thank God.

Both: (Katherine & Lauren) Yes, we are. (Lauren acting like nothing has happened)

Katherine: Thanks to God, your parent and me in particular your sister would have commit suicide.

Dylan: What?! sis? (Looking at her sister's face)

Lauren: Don't mind her, let's go in now! (Dylan and Irene still surprise)

Dylan: Ah, yes we are coming.

Lauren: walk before me (she pulled the rear wheels, the push rings swiftly rolled). Great, how does it feel to be back home thanks to Katherine I could have been dead by now. Only God knows.

Katherine: Only God knows?! Lauren: but thanks to you!

Dylan: So, Sister Katherine was not joking the other time about you committing suicide. But why? Even God says Suicide is a great sin.

Lauren: (she pretends like she doesn't know what they are saying) Oh, what shall we eat for lunch this great afternoon?

Irene: maybe, yam and eggs.

Dylan: That's not too bad.

Katherine: Lauren, have some rest lend your kitchen to me for today.

Irene: Wow, sister Katherine I know you have a great cooking skill and I cannot wait to eat your food!

Lauren: Whatever! (smiling and Turning to her room).

Katherine: Ok. (45 minutes after) Lauren, Dylan, Irene open could you girls come out? food is ready I have put everybody's food on the dinner table. Let's eat.

Dylan and Irene: (both answering with thin voice) we're coming.

Lauren: Too soon Katherine, but coming.

Katherine: No time for complain just come out of your room and eat, that's all I ask of.

Lauren: Okay (she opens her room door) Are you satisfy? Let's taste that food you are coasting of. It may not be that delicious.

Katherine: Gateman! Gateman!!, oh where did the gateman go now? let me recall his name Ah, got it Des-Des-Desmond! Desmond!!

Desmond: Yes madam (answered).

Katherine: Come! Here is your food, take it.

Desmond: Thank you, ma.

Irene: Your food is more delicious than sister Laurens' own.

Lauren: mmmuhm! Then let's my friend come over and leave with us so that you can eat her delicious food every day!

Katherine: don't get upset Lauren. ahn ah (looking at the screen of her cell phone)! My mum is calling, guess I have to take my leave.

Dylan: But!

Katherine: Don't worry, everything will be fine.

Lauren: ok, bye see you at school, ah (she turned the brakes) when are we resuming?

Katherine: hmmm, 28 of April 2010.

Lauren: ok! See you soon I may come visit.

Irene: could you take us with you whenever you want to go?

Lauren: okay.

Katherine: That is quite a promise.

Lauren: i know.

Katherine: Alright, Bye, come visit soon (receiving call) hello ma. I Am on my way (she inserts her key to the car) car beeps. (Dylan, Irene and Lauren wave at her).

****

ACT TWO

Happiness
(MR GILBERT BACK FROM TRAVELLING)

(Katherine got to the front of the gate, she blasted the car horn, the gateman rushed out of her house to get the gate opened. Katherine drove into the compound and park the car at her usual packing space. She heads straight to the entrance door and went inside) (Katherine's mom, Mrs. Edna Gilbert cut in)

Mrs. Edna Gilbert: Where have you been? your dad is worried.

Katherine: Dad? (looking surprised) is my dad back from traveling?

Mrs. Gilbert: Yes, it's quite some years now, shouldn't he return?

Katherine: He should, but we got no notice from him that he's coming back home.

Mrs. Gilbert: I guess this is the surprise he used to tell us about on the phone.

Mr. Myles Gilbert: Daughter (with his arms spread).

Katherine: (she embraced her dad) dad, you're welcome back (excited voice).

Mr. Gilbert: Wow (looking at Katherine), my daughter is now grown up. Katherine, I learnt in years to come now you are graduating from the university.

Katherine: Dad, in quite a year? (she asked and nod her head) It's not, it is quite in some months.

Mr. Gilbert: Ok! It worth celebrating, ah, how is your friend Lauren? I learnt that her parents had passed on. Hope she is coping well with her two younger ones?

Katherine: She is fine and well, that's where am coming from.

Mr. Gilbert: You're serious? wow, that good, when next you visit her extend our greetings to her and her younger ones, uhm?

Katherine: Yes dad, (she smiled). Dad when are we holding that party, I can't wait to hear that date.

Mr. Gilbert: Now of course but something is missing.

Katherine: What is that, dad? (laughs) uhm dad what is missing (in excitement voice).

Mr. Gilbert: uhm!!!

Katherine: Dad (so eager to hear it)!!!

Mrs. Gilbert: you mean, her fiancee?

Mr. Gilbert: Of course, you catch on quickly my dear.

Mrs. Gilbert: I forgot to tell you, she had already brought one home, he is quite intelligent, hard-working and besides, he already has his own Business, house and other properties. His name is Daniel King.

Mr. Gilbert: Wow, am more surprise. What are we still waiting for, let's call the party on immediately, and call your elder sister and your brother.

Katherine: Ok, Dad (she was so happy).

Mrs. Gilbert: Katherine!!!

Katherine: Yes, ma!!

Mrs. Gilbert: Your elder sister and her husband had already traveled today, it might not be easy to get in touch, besides i have informed them about your fiancee, uhm let's call her younger brother and your friends including Lauren.

Mr. Gilbert: Ok, its fine why not, I have missed a lot since all these years. How many years had it been.

Katherine: 6 years to be exact!

Mr. Gilbert: 6 years?

Katherine: Yes dad, you left immediately after my elder sister's wedding

Mr. Gilbert: Ah, I remembered, now let's start and discuss later.

(Party on)

(Lauren and her younger sisters have arrived at Katherine house, food is surplus, so is

drinks. The music is a bit loud to be called a celebrating party.)

(Kathrine fiancée, Daniel king walked in to the house and sat on the available sitting space. Daniel king owns a real estate company.)

Lauren: Wow, your dad is amazing, calling a celebration party after a long journey, six years!

Katherine: You remember that clearly? You have a great memory. Lauren, could you please excuse me, Daniel is around.

Lauren: yea sure (winking her eyes)

Katherine: (walking towards Daniel and spreading her harms requesting for a hug). Thank you for coming my love. What would you like to eat? There is Party jollof, your favorite, Fried rice and chips. Choose your choice my darling, I will get you nice drink with it.

Daniel: (smiling). Thank you, but I think only drink will do.

Katherine: come on, are you sure you are not hungry?

Daniel: yea, I just had my food before coming over.

Katherine: alright, I will get you the drink right away. Will be back in few minutes. (she fetched the drink and gives it to Daniel). Daniel!

Daniel: yes babe.

Katherine: I need to attend to Lauren and her sisters. I will be back shortly (she left).

Irene: Sister Katherine, is that your fiancée? (she asked) He's handsome.

Katherine: Thanks Irene.

Lauren: Has he introduced you to his parent.

Katherine: Yes.

Lauren: What of introduction between the two families? (asking with smile on her face)

Katherine: Lauren! That could not happen now, especially the state you are in. Do you think it's possible for me to engage or do introduction without you finding a suitor yet?

Lauren: What are you saying? Mtcheeew (she hissed), It would be fun coming to your wedding ceremony, won't it?

Katherine: Lauren!! (she throws a tantrum) (they laughed).

Irene: sister! sis!! (calling Lauren's attention).

Lauren: Yes, I am not deaf! what is it?

Irene: Ah, when are you going to introduce your fiancee to us (Katherine cuts in).

Katherine: don't you think this party is a little boring? Let's dance girls (music on).

****

ACT THREE

(THE JAMES FAMILY)

(Mr. and Mr.'s James are happily married for 28 years, they had two sons (Jacob and Barros). Barros is the eldest son, Jacob is Barros junior brother.)

(Mr. James is the owner of one of the Biggest pharmacies in the country, the Brand is well known all around.

Mr. & Mr.'s James had a fatal accident while driving to the Airport to catch their flight to UK. Mr. James sustain a lot of injuries, Mr.'s James, she hit her head on a very hard surface, her backbone and ribs was affected as well and she was unconscious for a long time. All other James were worried and frustrated, Mr.'s James was more frustrated, he thinks a lot about her wife, all these were too much for his body system and he died.)

(Mr. James first son (Barros) Travelled to Canada to complete his master's degree studies, Jacob was taking care of their mother (Mr.'s James) for months while she was still unconscious in the hospital.

Barros came back home from Canada to handle his father company after he completed his master's degree studies. When Barros got to the Airport, he ordered for a uber taxi from his cell phone to take him home.

Mr.'s James has gained her consciousness after months, Jacob is aware of his brother arrival, he is so eager to tell him about their mother).

Jacob James: (Calling) hello, Bro where are you right now?

Barros James: the uber I ordered ran out of fuel, we are at the filling station.

Jacob: some issues came up so you are needed, can you make it home soon?

Barros: I will try, but what is the main issue? at least give me clue ahn. You know I don't like suspense or surprises.

Jacob: It's about mom's health, I guess you can make it snappy bye! (hanged up)

Barros: hello! Hello!! Jacob. (confused). What has happened? I hope it's not what I'm thinking? Oh my God. Driver! Driver!!

Driver: yes oga.

Barros: what is delaying us? Please we need to move.

Driver: we are almost through oga, I just want to make sure I have my tank filled up to avoid delay like this. I am so sorry.

Barros: alright, no problem. Buh uhm, I have no time to waste, I have to get home quick. (uber driver start the car and drove out of the filing station).

(Arrival of Barros)

(The uber Driver hit the horn button on getting to the gate, he drove into the compound as the gateman opened up. Barros rushed out of the car, he ordered the gateman to get all his stuffs out of the car as he was having flash walk into the house. He opened the door and left it opened. He called his brother's name so loudly.)

Barros: Jacob! Jacob!!, (restless and nervous).

Jacob: (he came out walking gently) I am here bro.

Barros: are you serious? What exactly happened to mom?

Jacob: Calm down bro, Uhm, just guess what happened? (in exciting voice).

Barros: don't be such a girl Jacob, why guess? Am serious stop beating around the bush and go straight to the point and stop your useless jokes, uhm! (Jacob still excited and Bros shouted at him) Jacob! (he shouted) I wanna know Now!!!

Jacob: ah, mom, you know her, she…she…she (Barros move nervous and furious) is…is…free from her allergy and she can walk with her legs, ha, ha, ha, (laughs).

Barros: (stopped and looking at Jacob) what'd?

Jacob: stop starring Bro! I'm serious.

Barros: (slapping Jacob at face) hey Jacob! snap out of it, come on. You are joking right? (putting air out) hurh, am feeling heat is the air condition off? I am feeling heat, Jacob, go and on the air condition and repeat what you just said (putting out air more).

Jacob: oh god! (Jacob staring). (Clear his throat) hmm, the air condition is on so, stop being nervous and I said that mom's health is back, she is fine and sound like the olden days, that was my last words, satisfied?

Barros: (excited) seriously? (wrecking Jacob's cloth) you don't mean it? Oh, God at last mom is back.

Jacob: (Angrily) aish, ugh, stop that, you've just wrecked my cloth, so childish, seriously, follow me she is upstairs resting (footsteps approach).

Barros: Jacob, how long have she been up?

Jacob: two weeks ago, I'm sorry, I decided not tell you because I want you to concentrate on your studies. I knew you would want to come home when I tell you. (Jacob opened the door)

Mrs. James (Jacob and Barros mother): oh. You are here my son? Welcome. (her skin looked worn out and legs, walking with sticks).

Barros: (sobbing) mom, Jacob was just telling about your health, I am happy to see you.

Mrs. James: Don't worry, let's thank God my son. Jacob told me I have been unconscious for months. That aside, I haven't seen my husband for days in this house, where is your Dad?

Jacob: (furious) oh Dad? Dad (nervous and unable to explain) he...he (Barros cut in).

Barros: uhm, Dad? Let's leave that matter for now mum. We can catch on later, uhmn mother. He is on a trip right now, he will be back home soon.

Mrs. James: (curious) has something happened to my husband when am unconscious? uhmm?

Jacob: (deceiving their mother) no! of course no but let's talk later after you have a sound health uhmm mom!

Barros: Let's go, come on mum.

Mrs. James: You two haven't answered my question, yet I obey your orders to come upstairs, so obey mine too.

Barros: Ahhh (frustrated and touched his head)

Jacob: Mom? Can't you just…

Mrs. James: Just what ahn? Am sure you are not playing around again, correct! If you refused to answer me, I can get more information through many things, good night, bye (she banged and locked her door).

Jacob: Mom, open the door, please, we promise to tell you everything if only you will open your door (door opened).

Mrs. James: Promise Right? I have opened my door, so fulfill your promise and tell me what I need to know.

Jacob: ehm, uhm, uh, (scratching his head) about dad, uhm he is already… uh, Bros complete it.

Barros: Ah? Why should I Jacob? Continue your long story, uhm, young brother, you got this (scoff).

Jacob: You are really a coward brother. Ah, mom about dad, he's, hhum, he is already dea! dead.

Mrs. Jacob: Uhm? (looking at his two sons simultaneously) did I hear you clearly, repeat, what exactly happened? (stammering).

Jacob: Mom, you ask for it but to be more honest, Dad died of frustration and high blood pressure, since he thought you are going to die.

Mrs. James: Uhn! Uhn!! Uhn!!! (sobbing) hmmm (she fainted).

Barros: oh my God, See, see what you have caused!!

Jacob: Stop nagging and bring my car key from upstairs.

Barros: Are you commanding me now?

Jacob: Stop that already, mum is dying okay, so, let's continue the argument and neglect mom to die.

Barros: (furious and angry) aish! (walked down the steps) I drive and you watch mom at the back, okay.

Jacob: Okay! That's not a problem, just give me a hand. (shove his shoulder).

(At the hospital)

Barros: (facing doctor) How is she?

Doctor: She is okay, she just needs some rest that's all. But Mr. Barros, what exactly happened?

Jacob: she demands to know what happened to Dad, we had to tell her.

Doctor: Hell no, why would you do that while she is still in that condition?

Barros: we had no choice doctor, she was mad at us, we didn't want to tell her either.

Doctor: she could pass away because of the shock you know, but let's thank God. She is stable now.

Barros: Thanks to you doctor.

Jacob: yes, but Doctor, can we go in to see her.

Doctor: No! no!! no!!! let her rest for now, she seems distressed and worried.

Barros: really! Agh.

Doctor: I'm sorry, it's just for her to be fine, you will see her very soon. Excuse me please.

Jacob: its fine doctor, thank you so much.

Doctor: Yes. You're welcome (he walks away and face the receptionist) well-done.

Receptionist: Thank you, sir.

Jacob: I believe she will be fine, I will go get some stuffs for her, maybe you should stay in case.

Barros: alright, I will be here.

****

ACT FOUR

Reminiscence
(LAUREN IN HER MEMORY)

(It is the second semester of the final year, Lauren and her friend Katherine decided to live off campus. They both go to school from home and head back home after the lectures. Katherine suggested the idea so that Lauren can take care of her little sisters.)

(Dylan is in SS 3, she will write her west African Examination soon, Irene is in JSS 1, she just finished primary school Education.)

(Lauren finished her lecture before evening and she set to go home and called her driver for a ride, on getting to the house gate, Desmond opened the gate, the driver drove in, the car wheel and tyres stopped, the driver opened the car threshold, she gently sat on her wheelchair and went inside with her voice calling on her sister's name).

Lauren: Irene, Dylan (no answer). (she went out with ambulant) Desmond!

Desmond: (he rushed out answered) ma.

Lauren: where are my siblings?

Desmond: Ah, they've not returned from school, ma?

Lauren: really? (surprised), but they should have be in the house by now. Did it get this late before they close from school? (soliloquizing) (curious). Uhmm thanks Desmond, you may go back to your work (he returned and she went back inside) wow, how does it feel to be back home (she murmurs to herself and looks towards her parent's picture during this she remembered her parent).

Reflection (childhood memory)

(As Lauren was looking at the picture of her parent hanged on the wall of the sitting room, memory of her childhood came to her, she moved closer and bring down the picture. Her two parents were very caring and loving.)

(in the memory) Lauren was in primary 3 going to 4. End of the year party in her school is going on, Lauren won many prizes, she took the first position in her class, she made her parent very proud. Her father promised to buy her a new beautiful dress if she took first and she work towards it. Her father bought the beautiful dress for her as promised, her mother also bought a surprise present for her as well).

Late Mr. Leonard: Lauren, her is your present for taking the first position.

Young Lauren: oh daddy (she was happy), it's beautiful. Thank you, Daddy.

Late Mr. Leonard: go wear it (looking at her as she went to her mother).

Young Lauren: Mom, see, dad bought me a new dress, so does he buy yours too and Dylan?

Late Mrs. Leonard: Yes, he bought ours too, come, I also bought things from work to congratulate you on your promotion to primary four (4), you make us look the best of all in front of all parents, we love you dear (she kissed her on her cheeks) uhm-muah (young Dylan crying) let me attend to your younger sister (Dylan).

Young Lauren: mom, I'm gonna go wear it now. (she left for her room)

(5 Years After & The Birth of Irene)

(After two female children (Lauren & Dylan), Mrs. Leonard is pregnant with the third female child (Irene). The pregnancy wasn't easy for her, she's done series of medical test, Doctor keep telling her that things will be back to normal when the baby is out.)

(On one sunny Afternoon, the baby kicked her so hard to tell her it's time for her to come to life. It was very disturbing, she couldn't endure anymore, it was only her at

home, Mr. Leonard has gone to work, the two little Leonard has gone to school as well, she screams the name of the gateman, he was very scared seeing her in the state, he called Mr. Leonard cell phone to inform him if his wife condition. Mr. Leonard had a flash movement to his home in less than 5 minutes, he ordered his gateman to give hand in carrying his wife into the car. When he drove through the hospital gate, he applied brake, he rushed out, he called on the Nurses.)

(The nurses bring out the carriage wheel. Mrs. Leonard was place on it and taken to the labour room of the Hospital. She was in labour pain, he husband could not withstand seeing in her the state as well, he was walking from angle of the hospital to the other. He was dragging every Nurse coming from the labor room to ask about his wife condition. Mrs. Leonard is about to deliver, the Nurses were heling her.)

Nurses 1: Push, push harder madam, this is not your first nor second try to push harder please.

Late Mrs. Leonard: (laboring/crying). I'm trying nurse, I am getting tired.

Nurse 1: please I need you to keep trying, the baby is almost out, just push little more.

Late Mrs. Leonard: (she groaned very hard, the baby came out).

Nurse 2: there we go madam, (carrying the baby) congratulation, you just give birth to a beautiful baby girl. Congratulations once again.

Late Mrs. Leonard: (breathing heavily) thank you Jesus.

Nurse 2: we will go and clean the baby right away and you will be able to carry her. (she walked away with the new born).

Nurse 1: Madam! I will go out to inform your husband, I will be back shortly to clean you up. (she went out to tell Mr. Leonard about her wife safe delivery).

Mr. Leonard was still worried, he's unrest, raising and rubbing his two hand in prayer to God

Nurse 1: Sir? (tapped him from behind)

Late Mr. Leonard: (stammering and worried) yes?! Has my wife given birth? Is it a boy or a girl?

Nurse 1: congratulations sir, it is a bouncing beautiful baby girl just like her mom.

Late Mr. Leonard: (excited) yes! Uhmn, may I see her now? please

Nurse 1: yes, you may come with me now, sir! (they both went inside).

Late Mr. Leonard: oh my darling, are you alright?

Late Mrs. Leonard: i am fine (giving mild smile).

Late Mr. Leonard: any pain or ache anywhere?

Late Mrs. Leonard: not at all, I am fine.

Late Mr. Leonard: Nurse, where is the baby?

Nurse 1: oh, she has been taken away for clean-up, the other nurse that assisted me will bring her in soon. And pls sir, I need to clean your wife as well, so you will have to go out now, I will call you when we are done.

Late Mr. Leonard: alright nurse.

(After cleaning the Baby and the mother, Mr. Leonard was called into the ward to meet them both, they were discharged when it was confirmed that both the mother and Baby are in good health.)

(Some Months Before Their Demise)

(Mr. Leonard & Mrs. Leonard call on their eldest daughter and her sisters to discuss their plan to travel out of the country very soon on.)

Late Mr. Leonard: Lauren my, Dylan and Irene, it won't be long, your mom and I wish to travel abroad to check on our health (facing Lauren) and Lauren since you are the eldest, you will take care of your younger ones, correct?

Lauren: correct, sir! Salute, Lauren Leonard at your service (laughs) that's my Dad.

Late Mr. Leonard: That's my girl.

Lauren: may the lord grant you journey mercy and give you both sound health.

Late Mr. Leonard: but I am very hungry now, what shall we eat for dinner tonight.

Late Mrs. Leonard: mmhm, Lauren! What about you prepare pounded yam and vegetable soup.

Lauren: Yes, ma'am. I am on it right away.

(Next Day at Shoprite Mall)

(The Leonards set out to go shopping at Shoprite Mall, though initiated by the Late Mr. Leonard. Around the mall, there are other shop spaces occupied by other brand and individuals. There is playing ground for children, Game center, Restaurant, swimming pool and viewing center.)

Dylan: Dad, why are we here, there is enough stuff at home.

Late Mr. Leonard: yea, I know.

Irene: Mom, buy me that toy (pointing at the toy).

Late Mrs. Leonard: (surprise and sensitive) wait!

Irene: Mom buy me this….. (Irene interrupting).

Late Mrs. Leonard: Shhhhhh!! (shutting her)

Late Mr. Leonard: Why are you shushing your daughter?

Late Mrs. Leonard: Lauren!!!

Late Mr. Leonard: And What about her?

Late Mrs. Leonard: She is not here Darling.

Late Mr. Leonard: (looking around) oh my God, where is she?

Late Mrs. Leonard: (nervous and angry) she is missing, I mean Lauren is missing, I can't see her around. Oh my God.

Late Mr. Leonard: what should we do?

Late Mrs. Leonard: I don't know (confused).

(Mr. Leonard ran to the nearest security man)

Late Mr. Leonard: Hello sir, please we are looking for our daughter, she is not familiar with this place, please help us radio your other colleagues to look around.

Security: alright Mr., calm down. Can you tell me the type of dress she is wearing and the color?

Late Mr. Leonard: yea, she is wearing a Blue jean Trouser and white Round neck top wear.

Security: ok Mr. (Picking the communication Radio) Attention! Attention!! All guards and securities should be at alert, no car or individual should move out till Miss Lauren Leonard is found, all unit should stay on guards and search for Miss Lauren Leonard from your point, she is wearing a round Neck top wear and Blue Jean trouser. Over?

Lauren: (swimming at the swimming pool floor) uhmn! (she swims out) seriously! (she dressed up) oh, it seems they thought am lost, oh my God, am I still a baby, ahn? (curious and angry at herself, she went to her parent) mom? Dad? What's going on?

Mrs. Leonard: Oh my God! Where have you been? You have worried us.

Late Mr. Leonard: hey Lauren, what did you think you are doing? Where have you been? We have been looking for you over an hour, the security have searched everywhere.

Lauren: (murmurs) am not a kid anymore.

Dylan: what did you say sister Lauren?

Lauren: Nothing (giving Lauren her a weird look).

Mrs. Leonard: Where did you go? We are….(she is short of words)

Lauren: Mom, Dad, am not a baby anymore, I just went to swim that's all.

Security: Ma'am and Sir, we…(looked at Lauren) is this her? (Pointing at Lauren)

Mr. Leonard: here she is sir, thank you, we already recognize your service.

Security: why would you leave without telling your Mom or Dad? Alright sir, I will leave now (he went back to his post)

Mr. Leonard: I think we are done here, let's go home. (they went ack into their car and left the mall)

(When they got home, Lauren knew her father was very upset at her because of the scene she caused at the mall, she wants to make sure that he's no longer upset.)

Lauren: What did you want me to cook Mom, Dad?

Mrs. Leonard: Before that don't you think you, should apologize for what you did at the mall? Don't you?

Lauren: Dad, Mom, am very sorry but am no more a baby.

Mrs. Leonard: Lauren!!

Lauren: I Am sorry ma'am, sir, it will never repeat itself again. Dad what shall we have for supper? perhaps yam and egg?

Mr. Leonard: okay, that's my girl (his arm spread).

Lauren: Thanks Dad (embracing her dad).

Mrs. Leonard: Now, go and cook our supper.

(The Last Seen)

(Mr. & Mrs. Leonard are set for their trip to Abroad, they have their flight to catch by 11am in the morning, all their bags have been taken out of their room by their children.)

Mr. Leonard: hey Lauren! (placing hand on her shoulder) take care of the home and your sisters, we won't be long, we're going for just two weeks.

Mrs. Leonard: I will get you girls dresses from England ok. Be safe. (she hugged them one after the other)

Irene: I want to follow you (she wants to cry).

Mrs. Leonard: no Irene, we will back soon, but I promise you go next time. Even if you want to go now, it's too late, no travelling papers for you. I will get all those ready for next time.

Dylan: we will miss both. It feels like you are going forever.

Mr. Leonard: Dylan. It's just two weeks trip for us, ok? (facing Lauren) take this #30,000(thirty thousand Naira), this should do before we come back.

Lauren: thank you Daddy.

(Mr. & Mrs. Leonard hop into the car and drove to the airport, their children wave to them as they leave.)

(Mr. & Mrs. Leonard got into conversation as they drove to the airport.)

Mr. Leonard: My dear wife (he gave a glance look), I wish after our return we should celebrate our 23rd year of our marriage, don't you think?

Mrs. Leonard: hmmm, of course (she smiled). It's a nice idea.

Mr. Leonard: don't you think we should change the paint of the house, it's been five years we painted.

Mrs. Leonard: those paints still look good, we'll do that later, lets focus on the anniversary.

Mr. Leonard: I am also thinking Lauren should go for master's degree in London after her first degree. What did you think?

Mrs. Leonard: wow, she will be very happy to hear this from you.

(Everything black out, it feels like sleeping, every object was duplicating in the eyes of Mr. Leonard, he didn't know where he was. A long vehicle carrying gas lost control, probably brake failure had crushed their SUV jeep from behind and beyond survival. Other people around were at first afraid to move closer to the accident scene, there could be an explosion. Mr. & Mrs. Leonard were taken out of the crushed car forcefully, Mrs. Leonard isn't breathing anymore, Mr. Leonard still had pulse but has blood all over him, they were both rushed to the hospital in a good Samaritan vehicle.)

(Hospital)

(The two Leonard were place on different bed in the emergency ward. The doctor noticed that Mrs. Leonard is already dead, effort was made to safe Mr. Leonard as well, but he's lost too much of blood. The doctor ordered the Nurses to search Mr. & Mrs. Leonard body is there could be any means of identification which can be use to trace their relatives. Fortunately, Mr. Leonard wallet was found in his soaked trouser pocket, an identity card was found and which has the name & phone number of Lauren as the next of kin on the back. A call was put through to her.)

Doctor: (phone ring) Hello, am I speaking with Lauren?

Lauren: yes, this is Lauren, who is this please?

Doctor: my name is Doctor Teddy from MedLife Hospital, please we will like you to come over.

Lauren: what is going please?

Doctor: miss, it's actually nothing so serious, just come over. (he hanged up)

(Lauren Hurriedly grabbed the car key from the table)

Dylan: sister Lauren, what is happening? who was that?

Lauren: (she's nervous) it's a doctor from MedLife hospital, he asked me to come over.

Dylan: to come over for what?

Lauren: I don't know. You what, I will be back soon, you girls should wait for me.

Dylan: no! let's go together. Irene, come on, we're going out.

Irene: are we going to the cinema?

Dylan: no, not now. We will go later. Let's move sister. (they drove to MedLife hospital)

(On getting to MedLife hospital, Lauren move towards the Nurse at the reception Desk. She requested to see the doctor.)

Doctor: welcome, you're Leonard Lauren?

Lauren: yes Doctor. What is going on?

Doctor: Hmmm, sorry miss, but if I may ask, what relation do you have with Mr. Leonard?

Lauren: I am her Daughter, these are my siblings.

Doctor: alright, its fine. Miss Lauren, hmmm, I will like you to be calm ok.

Lauren: alright, go on please (not in a calming voice)

Doctor: Three hours ago, Mr. Leonard and a woman but I presume his wife were brought to our facility here, their car was crushed by a Gas vehicle that loose control and hmm as our work, we tried so hard to safe them but our effort was futile, I am sorry, we loose them both.

Lauren: (silent for some seconds) doctor, I don't understand.

Doctor: I need you to be strong, hmmm, your parents are dead.

Lauren: nooooo!!! Doctor no, this can't be through, noooooo! (crying so loud)

Doctor: miss you need to take heart, please do not injure yourself.

Lauren: (still crying) alright doctor, alright (breathing heavily and shedding tears). Where are they, I need to see them.

Doctor: yes, you will see them, that is the only reason we haven't taken them to the morgue. Follow me please.

(Dylan and Irene were sitting at the reception, they saw Lauren and the Doctor walking out of the office, Lauren was still shedding tears, Dylan rushed and moved closer to her sister to know what has happened.)

Dylan: hey sis, what is wrong, why're you crying? Talk home. (walking by Lauren side, holding her arm and looking at her face)

Lauren: follow me, where is Irene?

Dylan: she is over there (Irene is too young to know what is happening)

Lauren: go bring her.

(The doctor opened the door of the ward where Mr. & Mrs. Leonard dead body are lying)

Lauren: Mom, Dad, No!! uh No! No!!(looking at her parent on the hospital bed) (in tears). Dad! Mom! Please don't leave us.

Dylan: oh my God (placing her two hand on the head) No, mum, dad. (crying heavily). Why? God why?

Irene: Sister Lauren, what's going on, why is dad and mom sleeping on this bed? Let's bring them back home (still young and can't understand)

(Extant)

(Lauren weeping and crying as she holds her parent's picture)

Lauren: No! (sobbing) uhm, uhm, uhm, uhm! Ha! (she screamed so loud) mom!! Dad!!

Desmond: (he rushed into the house) huhn! Miss (standing close to Lauren), what's wrong again? Why are you doing this to yourself Miss? Don't injure yourself please, you know it's just you for younger ones, Be strong for them. (Dylan and Irene walks in).

Dylan: sis! What's wrong? Mr. Desmond, what happened?

Desmond: (Shook head) I don't know, I heard her voice, so I came in and I saw her crying, you two also came in just in time. I should go back to the gate now.

Dylan: uhm! Irene go upstairs uhmn ok, I will join you soon, I need speak with sister Lauren

Irene: Why? What happen? why is sister Lauren crying? You said Mom and Dad traveled but why are they not returning? (so sensitive) and sister Lauren is here holding their picture with bunch of tears to full a bucket. Talk to me please, what is going on? Sister Lauren! Dylan!

Dylan: I said go upstairs (she nagged).

Irene: Don't nag at me just answer my question and that will be all (she also Nagged)

Dylan: And you have the gut to face me and disrespect me?

Irene: Aish. (touching her forehead).

Lauren: can you two stop all this nagging? This is no time for all these, Irene, can you go to upstairs please, don't worry everything will be fine.

Irene: alright sister Lauren (leaving).

Lauren: Irene!

Irene: (looked back) yes sister.

Lauren: I don't like you disrespecting you sister, the way you acted now is improper and I need you to apologize to her, ok?

Irene: alright sister. I am sorry Dylan.

Dylan: its fine little sis. (Irene went away). (turned to her sister) sister Lauren, is this the time for this? You are expected to be strong for the two of us and not the way you are sister. Please we don't wanna loose you too.

Lauren: Dylan, I understand everything you said, it just that memory carry me away, I don't know when I started crying. Come here (she hugged Dylan)

****

ACT 5

Discussion

(DISCUSSION AMONG THE GILBERT FAMILY)

Mr. Gilbert: Isn't it the right time now to set your wedding ceremony or wife what do you think?

Mrs. Gilbert: Wedding? How can that come first without introduction between the two families, don't be ridiculous.

Katherine: Mom, Dad. Am not through with my education yet, you are already thinking of introduction and wedding. Ah, I can't believe you two are doing this.

Mr. Gilbert: I thought the faster the better but I was wrong. All of all, when will you be ready, I really wish to see my grandchildren that will call me grandpa and will dis-organize this house while crawling uhm… my daughter please you and your fiancee should make it snappy since you've already brought him home. well, I can't wait till we meet his parent for the introduction and set your wedding day, ah, you said your fiancee's name is….(recollecting).

Katherine: Daniel!! His name is Daniel, father.

Daniel: (car horned) open the gate please.

Gateman: who is there?

Daniel: it's me Daniel, Katherine's fiancee.

Gateman: Coming sir (with food in his mouth) please bear with me (chewing) I'm sorry (gate opens).

Daniel: No, problem, is she home?

Gateman: Yes, she is sir.

Katherine: (she looked out of the window to see who's coming) talk of the devil, darling dude (amaze tone).

Mr. Gilbert: Not bad.

Daniel: (knocked on the door)

Katherine: come in, the door is unlocked.

Daniel: (he opened the door and walked in) Good evening sir and ma'am.

Mrs. Gilbert: good evening Daniel, have your seat.

Mr. Gilbert: Evening Daniel, hmmm, your fiancee (Katherine) said until she is through with her education and secure a job before getting married, is that true?

Daniel: Ah, sir, i am confused.

Katherine: (laughs) uhm!

Mr. Gilbert: Katherine! Why are you laughing?

Mrs. Gilbert: Your fiancee (Katherine) said till she finished her education she can marry or wed. Is that true? Enlighten us more.

Daniel: Uhm, Katherine (then turn his eyes around) thanks to her, my future plan is delayed.

Mr. & Mrs. Gilbert: Thanks to who?

Daniel: Katherine!

Mr. Gilbert: Katherine! So, the decision was made by you alone without your fiancee consent and agreement, oh my God.

Katherine: Yes, he can change that if only he has proposed but he didn't, so my decision remains firm.

Mrs. Gilbert: Really? (facing Daniel).

Daniel: uhm! I haven't because I thought you may turn me down and I don't really like disappointment.

Mrs. Gilbert: You should have given it a try and you would have had a reasonable explanation to give right now.

Katherine: I won! Wow! I won, won, won (scoff and laughs).

Daniel: Ah, sir, ma'am! I wish to inform you that I want to take your daughter to a launching party, if I may?

Mr. Gilbert: that's not a problem? And do something about the proposing deeds, okay.

Daniel: Yes sir, Katherine come on.

Katherine: Right now? You are joking, you should have informed me earlier. look at me, what did you see?

Daniel: You are dressed, and the dress is fine for the outing.

Katherine: correct! Have dressed up which means I got somewhere else to go, bye! (she stood up) Dad, mom I wish to visit Lauren, it's been a while now that I have seen her (heading out).

Mr. Gilbert: Come back here right now (commanding her) you are going out with Daniel.

Katherine: ahh, Dad.

Mrs. Gilbert: Isn't your father talking to you? Moreover, aren't you resuming back next week, why visiting her again?

Mr. Gilbert: (hiss) aren't you going to school on Monday? and you still want to visit her, we disagree, you are going nowhere.

Katherine: But Dad!

Mrs. Gilbert: (scoff) uhm.

Daniel: (worried) Katherine! you may go, please, sir, ma'am, I beg on her behalf. Let her go.

Mr. Gilbert: I have Already given her order, it is either she go out with you or she stay back inside.

Katherine: (She angrily walk upstairs) aish! (her room door opened and closed) he messed things up (she picked up her phone and dial Lauren's number).

Lauren: (Phone beeps) hello! Katherine.

Katherine: i am sorry I won't be able to make it over there.

Lauren: Not to worry sweetie, uhm.

Katherine: Okay bye. See you next week in school (conversation ends).

Irene: (curious) is she coming?

Lauren: (disappointed) no, she isn't?

Dylan: (curious) why? But she promised.

Lauren: Don't know. Let's go out by ourselves, okay.

Mrs. Gilbert: (knocking Katherine's door) Katherine, Katherine, eh, you better come out and escort you fiancee.

Katherine: (snoring and pretending to be asleep).

Daniel: Okay, ma'am I will take my leave.

Mrs. Gilbert: Okay, Sorry Daniel, uhm may be another day you two can go out because she is already sleeping (she escorted him out). Ok, bye (gate open and closed).

Mr. Gilbert: (Katherine's dad knew she pretend to be asleep and was agitated) You better stick to your room like gum and never come out cos i am very mad at you, you disrespected me in the presence of your fiancee! (he stood up to go to his room)

Katherine: (she opened her door) dad! mom! Am really sorry but I can't follow him and obey your wish I will rather stay in my room than follow him to that party or whatever.

Mrs. Gilbert: My daughter, you shouldn't have, see your father is angry and almost bumped into fire, his eyes is as red as pepper ready to harm anyone.

Katherine: (run to catch up with her Dad) Dad! (holding his legs) please forgive me, am sorry for disobeying you but if I do and follow him, Lauren and I might bump into each other, what do I do? Should I tell her that you forced me to follow him and break our agreement. I am so sorry Dad.

****

ACT SIX

Trust and fate

(GETTING OVER DEPRESSION)

(Lauren and her two sisters were discussing what could have prevented Kathrine from coming to their house, It was forgotten and they head out to have fun)

Irene: I wonder what happened that she couldn't make it.

Dylan: I can't even think of anything either.

Lauren: maybe we should check on her.

Dylan: I disagree.

Irene: why? It's better to check on her health and stop assuming!

Dylan: maybe she and her fiancee went out or her parent order her not to go out, either one of the two (she nods).

Lauren: She seems alright and no vehicle interrupted but I can hear some ruckus sound.

Dylan: I guess the other side is right.

Lauren: Other side?

Dylan: Yes, maybe her parent didn't allow her to come.

Lauren: That's not possible.

Dylan: Remember I said maybe.

Irene: Maybe Dylan is right.

Lauren: if that's right, let assume her parent didn't allow her to go out, but would they?

Irene: uhm! I thought as much (she nods).

Dylan: oh, her parents her funny, human being forget this quote which says delay isn't denial though a vision tarries, wait for it. It shall come to pass.

Lauren: You mean? (curious).

Dylan: Her parents are looking down on you,

Lauren: that's not possible. Let's stop all these please.

Irene: That's no possible Dylan, sister Lauren! her parent likes you and cannot look down on us, right.

Dylan: Have you forgotten already? never trust others, their loyalty varies, oh, it's getting late Sis, let's go to park or art gallery either of the two.

Lauren: Art gallery!

Irene: No way, park! Sis, please let's go to park uhm! Park, park, park!

Lauren: Aish! You are too noisy alright, park? Fine.

Irene: (excited) yes! (she folds her hands) thanks sis (they walked by Lauren wheel's chair towards their car).

Lauren's driver: Desmond!! Desmond!! Open the gate and stop assuming.

Desmond: ok. (gate opened, he peeped through the glasses to talk to Lauren in the car) buy me something too.

Dylan: Like what?

Desmond: Uhm, fried rice and chicken.

Lauren: Okay, you can count on it.

Desmond: Thank you sister Lauren.

Lauren: Sister? Am I your sister? (she hissed).

Desmond: Don't be offended, am sorry!

Lauren: Bye,

Dylan: Till evening Desmond.

Irene: Bye sir.

Desmond: bye little Irene.

****

ACT SEVEN

(DESTINY WILL SURE PREVAIL WHEN THERE IS HOPE)

(Background music as they approach the gate of the park, its weekend, many other parents came with their children, the crowd is much, Lauren didn't like too much of crowd, she exhale as she saw the crowd)

Dylan: Wow, I love this song! (expressing her feeling to her sister).

Lauren: We are here! Let's have fun.

Irene: (excited) ah! Thanks sis (she loves the crowd she was seeing).

Dylan: The premises is beautiful.

Lauren: yea, that's true but I don't like too much of crowd

(A guy bumped into her wheelchair) ah! Oh my God (she looked up).

Jacob: I am so sorry! (he apologized).

Lauren: (angry) oh!! You are? You stain my dress! Can sorry clean it up?

Dylan: (she pinched her) sis! Leave him, (she whispered) let's get your cloth clean first.

Lauren: aish, my dress is so stained (she hissed irritatedly).

Jacob: (silently) but Why is she so upset! After all I've apologized to her (he hissed and walked away).

Lauren: (In their car) he stained my dress, he embarrassed me in public, we haven't even gotten into the main part of the park.

Dylan: parasites? Those are human beings not parasites, sis! Stop this let's go (she turned to Irene) Irene! it was your idea to come here!

Irene: ah? I don't know this would happen. sis, There, Over there! It seems you can buy a new dress and change right there besides it is very exclusive and I think we brought enough cash to tush up, right? Why not you buy another dress instead of doing cleaning, the cleaning will even take much time.

Dylan: ok, sis, stop feeling embarrassed and let's go over there (pointing at the exclusive shop).

Lauren: exclusive shop? That means only few and important people who has access to hotel or companies has the audacity to go in, right?

Irene: Yes! And we are exactly like that, um!

Lauren: ok, let's go. (The driver turned the car in direction of the shop)

Shop Assistant (Rose): ma'am (smiling), what can we do for you?

Lauren: we want to buy a dress

Shop Assistant (Rose): do you have a choice? Welcome sir (she greeted Jacob)

Lauren: umh! (she looked around) I want this dress, pink...! Uhn. (he saw Jacob) you? why are…! Are you following us around?

Jacob: why would i do that? You look surprised right? Ok, I owned this place, this is my shop, or would you still wanna know why I am here? Hey, hello (snapped his finger)

Lauren: (speechless) um!

Jacob: (he scoffs) I can see you came here to change your dress and make up since I caused it. Rose, please provide her all her needs on my behalf.

Shop Assistant (Rose): Yes sir. Ma'am, you said you like the pink?

Lauren: Yes. (she smiled)

Irene: sis (she looked surprised)!!

Dylan: Let's go.

Lauren: Lead the way I'll follow you.

Shot Assistant (Rose): okay Ma'am.

Jacob: Lauren, I will be waiting for you right outside. your sisters can as well pick what they like.

Lauren: thank you.

Dylan: this is surprising I must say (smiling).

Irene: me too (smiling).

(Lauren and her sister are done picking from the shop, they were heading out.)

Lauren: you girls should mind the glasses (wheeling towards the front door of the shop).

Jacob: (leaning his body on the car) hey, did you pick all you want?

Lauren: (she rolled casters towards Jacob) having the free will to pick what I want should not turn too greediness. Hey, thank you.

Jacob: I just pay for my mistake, so don't thank me. My name is Jacob (stretching his hand for handshake).

Lauren: (shaking hands) I am Lauren. (she turned the wheels towards her sisters) Dylan, you and your sister should wait for me in the car.

Dylan: thank you Jacob.

Irene: thank you.

Jacob: (smiling and waving at Irene & Dylan as they leave). You're welcome. Lauren, I'll like to apologize for staining your dress, it's as a result of rushing to meet a friend.

Lauren: its fine, after all, you have paid for the new dress (both laughed).

Jacob: (smiling) yea. Lau hmm, Lauren, right?

Lauren: (Smiling) yea.

Jacob: I will like to know more about you, do you mind telling me little about yourself?

Lauren: hmmm, I already told you my name, my parents are late, it's just me and my sisters right now, I am a final year student in the university, my Dad is the owner of Nass innovation group of company, my mum use to be a nurse, I think all these should do for now.

Jacob: yea, I'm so sorry about your parent. So, you re the daughter of the famous owner of Nass innovation in this this town? Wow, I'm crossing the line already, I guess.

Lauren: (smile) of course not.

Jacob: well, hmmm, I told you my name too (both laugh). My Dad is late, my mum is still in the hospital due to the shock from the accident she had with Dad. Mum was actually unconscious for period of hmmm, I can't really remember how long. My Dad is the owner of Abakad pharmacy in which my elder brother is now the CEO, I have degree in international marketing from the university of London and hmmm. I think that should also do about me.

Lauren: I'm so sorry about your Dad. Abakad pharmacy was what I heard right? I'm about to be blown away I must say. The number one producer of different medicine in the country.

Jacob: (smile) stop flattering me.

Lauren: you know I am not.

Jacob: hmmm, Lauren!

Lauren: yea!

Jacob: I have a request.

Lauren: alright, go on. What's that?

Jacob: can we both pay my mum a visit at the hospital?

Lauren: oh, yea. its fine, how about tomorrow, I'm free.

Jacob: that's ok. Thank you (mild smile). So, do you mind I giving me your cell phone number?

Lauren: yea sure, (dialing her number on Jacob cell phone).

Jacob: and how about I give you a walk to your car (he gently pushed Lauren's wheels towards the car).

Lauren: I should thank you once more for the dress and that of my sisters. Thank you.

Jacob: come on Lauren, drive safe ok.

Dylan: bye Jacob (Irene is already asleep in the car).

Jacob: (waving) bye Dylan. See you later.

Dylan: Well, before we leave remember we promised Uncle Desmond to get him something.

Jacob: Uncle Desmond?!

Irene: Uhn, he is our gate man.

Jacob: Ah! May I order it?!

Lauren: not to worry, I will do that on our way home. Thank you. Bye.

(Lauren Drove out)

Dylan: (clearing the throat forcefully**)** so, sister (she winked).

Lauren: (she smiled) so what? Naughty girl.

****

ACT EIGHT

(A VISIT TO JACOB MUM AT THE HOSPITAL)

(Lauren no longer leave her two sisters at home whenever she is going out, they are now her companion. They drove to the James house, they left to the hospital in Jacob Toyota venza jeep, it is a very big car.

When they arrive at the hospital, Jacob was leading the way to her mother's ward, a private ward though. He opened the door.)

Jacob: Mom!

Mrs. James: my son, welcome.

Jacob: how're you feeling? Are you alright now to move around?

Mrs. James: uhn Jacob, it's getting better, at least I can stand on my feet. (Lauren and her siblings appeared) who are you? (she said gently) Why are you here? Son, did you know them (looking at Jacob).

Lauren: I am.... (Jacob cuts in).

Jacob: Ah, mum, she is.... (he looked at Lauren's face).

Lauren: uhm, I am Lauren ma'am.

Mrs. James: alright, who are you? because I don't think I have seen these faces before.

Lauren: I am the daughter of Mr. & Mrs. Leonard. My parent owns (Jacob cut in again).

Jacob: Her parents own a company that worth 250 million Naira.

Mrs. James: I see But, Jacob

Jacob: yes mom.

Mrs. James: is she your girlfriend? Oh sorry, I shouldn't be asking that now. Lauren, you are not bad. But what happened to your legs, were you born this way?

Lauren: (smiled) No I wasn't, after my parents demised, the news was alarming and I was hospitalized for months, after regaining consciousness, my legs were paralyzed, (she narrated bitterly).

Mrs. James: oh! This is touching. I must thank you my darling. Thank you for coming. These are your siblings? right?

Lauren: yes ma'ma. This is Dylan, this is Irene (pointed at them one after the other)

Mrs. James: they are both cute.

Lauren: Irene, Dylan let's go.

Irene: sis!

Lauren: yes, Irene

Irene: I wish to climb the swing outside and play around a little.

Lauren: No! No!! let's go home.

Jacob: come on Lauren, she's just a little girl, let her play

Mrs. James: she needs it Lauren. Allow her.

Irene: sis! sis!! Please I promise to be fair.

Lauren: you have just 20 minutes Irene.

Irene: Yes, come let's have fun together uncle Jacob (she holds his hand and drag him along).

(There is playing ground for kids in the compound of the hospital, aside that, the hospital is a well sophisticated one, this makes it the main reason why the wealthy one In the city have chosen it.)

(Jacob and Irene got to the children playing ground, Jacob is helping Irene to move her swing. Lauren and Dylan enjoyed the serenity of the surrounding. Jacob asked Dylan if she could help Irene do the pushing of the swing.

Jacob then left to stand beside Lauren.)

Jacob: (standing beside Lauren). She loves the swing (referring to Irene).

Lauren: yea (she smiles). Thank you for helping her (she looked at Jacob face).

Jacob: Lauren! (he called her name holding her hand from side).

Lauren: (she wasn't resisting the holding of her hand instead she looked at his and answered). Yes (very softly).

Jacob: (looking down) hmmm, I've got something to say Lauren.

Lauren: ok. Go on. Speak. (looking at his face).

Jacob: (he exhaled) I don't know how to start.

Lauren: (smile) just start anyhow.

Jacob: hmmm. Maybe next time.

Lauren: you might not have next time bro.

Jacob: (smiled) Lauren!

Lauren: yea.

Jacob: i am not good at writing or saying epistle, I like to be straight forward. I've got feelings for you since the first time I met you at the park, I hmmm, I lack confidence when it comes to saying this. I like you Lauren.

Lauren: I like you too, its normal right?

Jacob: Lauren, I like you, I hmmm, I want you as my future partner (his body was shaking).

Lauren: (she understands too well, she was expecting this from him). Jacob!

Jacob: yea (he answered hurriedly).

Lauren: you've got to give me little time to think about it.

Jacob: it's no problem Lauren. I will wait to hear response from you. I will wait (he's a bit nervous,)

Lauren: I think we need to leave now.

Jacob: oh yea, you should. (he leaves Lauren Hand).

Lauren: hey Dylan, that's ok, let's go home.

Irene: no sis! Please more minutes.

Lauren: no! let's go home, it's getting late, we should go.

(Dylan stopped pushing and Irene jumped down, they both walked to their sister)

Jacob: I should drive you home so that you can take your car.

Lauren: oh, I've forgotten we parked at your house. (they hop into Jacob venza, he drove them home). Thank you, Mr. Jacob, we will now be on our way. (opening the car).

Jacob: wait! (he used his hand right hand to hold the car door and the second hand to touch her shoulder) wait!

Lauren: (she looked surprise) why?

Jacob: (he removed his hand) can you do me a favour?

Lauren: favour?

Jacob: Yes, can you give me your home address?

Irene: Yes!

Lauren: Irene!!

Irene: our address is….. (she called out).

Dylan: Irene, you are too much and straight forward (smiling).

Jacob: Thank you Irene.

Irene: My pleasure uncle Jacob. Thanks for helping me today.

Jacob: bye girls.

Lauren: bye (she drove out)

****

ACT NINE

(DANIEL IN A CONVERSATION WITH HIS FATHER)

(Daniel king father doesn't live in the same town with his father, his mother his late since he was 12 years hold, his father married kate after 4 years his mother died. Kate born 2 children for Daniel's father, a boy and a girl.)

(Daniel is the only child of his mother. He is very hard working and intelligent, he's old enough to get married, he called his father to tell him about Katherine, his fiancée.)

Daniel: (calling on the phone) hello Dad.

Daniel's dad: My son long time, what's wrong with you, your voice has changed. Are you ok?

Daniel: Nothing! Nothing, sir! Yes, I am fine, just waking up from my sleep sir.

Daniel's dad: Really? Are you sure?

Daniel: yes Dad, how is sister kate too?

Daniel's dad: She is fine and sound. She is in the kitchen cooking.

Daniel: alright sir.

Daniel Dad: When are you coming to visit us?

Daniel: Anytime from now, okay.

Daniel Dad: so, son, what is it this time?

Daniel: Yes, (smiling) I just wanted to hear your voice and discuss something with you.

Daniel's dad: what's that son?

Daniel: I wanted to tell you that I've found a suitor.

Daniel Dad: oh, finally, I am happy for you (smile) that means I will get to see my grandchildren soon.

Daniel: yes dad.

Daniel Dad: how far? Did you know any of her family?

Daniel: yes, I've been to her parent house and I've been accepted. So…….

Daniel Dad: that's good son, so you should bring her to me too.

Daniel: yes definitely. Will let you know sir.

Daniel Dad: alright son. You stay safe.

Daniel: Bye sir.

Daniel's dad: Bye, bye!

Kate: (she came out of the kitchen) was that Daniel?

Daniel Dad: oh yes.

Kate: why didn't you call me to speak with him?

Daniel Dad: sorry, he's coming to pay us visit with his finacee very soon.

Kate: wow, that nice, I'm happy for him.

****

ACT TEN

(JACOB VISIT TO LAUREN HOUSE)

(Jacob wanted to surprise Lauren and her sister, he holds the paper where he wrote the home address, he picked his car key from the home theatre shelf and he drove out of the compound.)

(On getting to Lauren Estate, he located the street written on the paper using planted sign board, he drove slowly till he gets to their gate, then he put a call through to Lauren.)

Jacob: (Phone ring) hello, what's up Lauren?

Lauren: hey Jacob, how are you?

Jacob: I'm very well. What about you?

Lauren: what's good?

Jacob: Goodness. Guess what?

Lauren; (smile) what is it Jacob? I am not good at doing that.

Jacob: I'm at your gate.

Lauren: what!! Oh my God, are you serious?

Jacob: I am serious, come check yourself, I am right here.

Irene: is that uncle Jacob?

Lauren: (smile) yea, it's him.

Dylan: (she winks to her sister**)** wow, here we go.

Lauren: Desmond!! Where is he?

Desmond: yes ma. I'm here. (he ran out of his room close to the gate)

Lauren: we have a visitor, kindly open the gate.

Desmond: alright ma. (he opened the gate for Jacob).

Jacob: (he drove into Lauren's compound**)** thank you (he thanked

Desmond as he get down from the car).

Irene: (she ran from inside the house to meet Jacob) welcome uncle Jacob, come, sister Lauren is inside (dragging him inside).

Lauren: (she sat on the sofa) welcome Jacob.

Dylan: welcome uncle Jacob.

(Irene sat beside Jacob, Lauren was sitting right opposite him, looking at each other straight feels so good. Jacob actually went visiting to get an answer from Lauren)

Lauren: what shall we offer you? You didn't tell us you are coming we would have prepared good delicacy before your arrival.

Jacob: I am ok, do not bother, I haven't come for food.

Dylan: (he understands too well what Jacob has come to do) we should excuse you two. Irene! Let's go watch Avtar in the room. (they left).

Lauren: why did you come visiting today with any notice.

Jacob: I actually did that on purpose (smiling).

Lauren: so, how is mom doing? how is her health?

Jacob: it much better, thank you. She also asked of you.

Lauren: so? Why re u in my home?

Jacob: I hmmm,

Lauren: you hmmm, ehn (mocking Jacob)

Jacob: I am here to get the response to my request from you Lauren.

Lauren: (she exhaled heavily and looked at Jacob eyes). Alright Jacob, but how do I know you are truly serious?

Jacob: this is very simple, I wouldn't be stressing myself if I am not serious and besides, I already told mummy about it and she likes you.

Lauren: Jacob!

Jacob: hey Lauren, i only need you to trust me. I will wait till you finish your education and we can have our wedding.

Lauren: alright, I've heard you. Your Request is granted.

Jacob: oh! You don't know how happy. I am the happiest man on earth today. Thank you Lauren and I promise to always make you happy.

Lauren: how is your Brother?

Jacob: oh, Barros? He's fine. (he smiles). He hardly have time for his life when he now became our father successor. I will take my leave now.

Lauren: oh, so soon?

Jacob: yea, I need to go see mum in the hospital.

Lauren: my regards to her.

Jacob: I will. Dylan! Irene! I will take my leave now.

Dylan: uncle Jacob, so soon?

Jacob: yea, where is Irene?

Dylan: she is already sleeping.

Jacob: alright. You give her own share to her when she wakes up (giving some cash to Dylan)

Dylan: thank you.

Lauren: thank you Jacob. I should see you off to your car (they moved out of the house and walked to Jacob car). Drive safe.

Jacob: alright darling (he winks)

Lauren: (she smiled**).** Desmond, open the gate.

(Jacob drove out waving at Desmond. Lauren went back inside.)

****

ACT ELEVEN

(GRADUATION DAY)

(it's convocation Day, it's a day of celebrate the completion of four years journey, Katherine and her Friend Lauren finished their studies with good Grades. All of the Graduating students were gathered in the school auditorium wearing the graduation Gown and cap.)

(it's just Lauren and her sister to celebrate the graduation, the memory of her parent wants to come to her head when she see other graduating student taking picture shot with their parent. Katherine is taking shot with her parent and siblings, Daniel is also present. Katherine called Lauren from afar to join her family)

Kathrine: hey Lauren! How are you? (she hugged her)

Lauren: hi Kathrine, I'm very well, how are you too? Good morning ma, good morning sir (greeting Katherine Parent).

Mr. & Mrs. Gilbert: Good morning Lauren.

Mr. Gilbert: how have you been darling? And how are your sisters?

Lauren: we are all good sir. Thank you.

Mrs. Gilbert: congratulations to you girls. We are very proud of you. I am sure your parent we be proud of you. Well-done.

Lauren: thank you ma.

Mr. Gilbert: I am sorry about your parent, I was out of the country when it happened.

Lauren: yea I know sir. Thank you.

Mr. Gilbert: come on let's take picture together.

Katherine: yea sure. Dylan! Irene!! come over here, let's take picture together. (Dylan & Irene move closer).

Katherine: (holding Daniel). Lauren! Meet Daniel my fiancée.

Lauren: hi Daniel (stretching her hand for a hand shake) finally, we meet, it's nice meeting you.

Daniel: the pleasure is all mine.

Lauren: we could not meet the last time. Guess you left early.

Daniel: yea, I got a call from my client. I had to leave.

Irene: hey sis, (very loudly and pointing at opposite direction) see uncle Jacob! He's here.

Lauren: (surprised) oh my God (placing her palm on her chest).

Jacob: Irene! Dylan!! How are you? (he moved closer to Lauren).

Lauren: Jacob! (still surprised) Don't know you can make it here.

Jacob: (he pecks Lauren) congratulations babe.

Lauren: (she hugged him) thank you for coming babe.

(Katherine standing and experiencing the whole drama)

Katherine: (she clear throat**)** Lauren?

Lauren: oh sorry, Jacob, meet Katherine, my very good friend I used to tell you.

Jacob: hi Kathrine, I'm happy to meet you, Lauren told me a lot about you. Thank you for always being there for her.

Katherine: it's my pleasure.

Lauren: Kathrine! This is my fiancée, we met not too long.

Katherine: come here (she hugged Lauren and whisper to her hear). I am happy for you my friend.

Lauren: (she also whispers to Katherine hear) thank you.

Katherinc: when are you leaving?

Lauren: probably when we have collected our certificate from the faculty.

Katherine: alright Lauren. We'll see later. Bye Jacob (waving at him).

Jacob: bye Katherine (he waved back at her). Dylan! Irene!! Let's take picture with your sister.

Lauren: after taking picture, I will need to move to the faculty for collection of my certificate from the HOD office.

Jacob: it's fine, I will drive you there.

Lauren: thank you babe.

Jacob: congratulation once again, (he Hugged her).

****

ACT TWELVE

(A MONTH AND HALF AFTER CONVOCATION)

(It's been 45 days after convocation, Lauren decided to visit Katherine in her parent house, she was going to discuss about the preparation of her wedding with Jacob)

(At Katherine's house)

Lauren: (knocking)

Katherine: Yes?

Lauren: It's me Lauren.

Katherine: Lauren! Come in, the door is unlocked.

Lauren: my friend, (she hugged Katherine).

Katherine: Long time no see, I've missed you, I called your number but switched off. I came over to your house but Desmond said you've gone out with your sisters. I was so worried because We didn't later see each other at the faculty on convocation day. Daniel too always asked of you.

Lauren: (she smiled) I have been ok Kathrine. Thank you.

Kathrine: so, what's the 411? (asking what she has come to do).

Lauren: Yes, it's good you know that I have come for a purpose. I learnt your wedding is next two month, mine too is next two month, the same date also.

Katherine: (in surprise) Really? Then let's do it together since we promised each other to wait and do our wedding the same time.

Lauren: that's why I am here, I remember let's go inside the other sitting room already.

Katherine: Come in (she smiled and feels excited).

Mr. & Mrs. Gilbert: Lauren?! Since these years, we missed you and we learnt you traveled without your friend's consult.

Lauren: Am sorry ma'am and sir, but I feel I have to let Katherine and her fiancee to have a nice time together so I won't be an hindrance between them and beside it wasn't my idea to travel it was my fiancee decision.

Mrs. Gilbert: Your fiancee?

Lauren: Yes ma'am.

Mrs. Gilbert: i am happy for you.

Lauren: Yes, ma'am, thank you. I learnt Katherine's wedding is next two month. It clash with mine and while we're in school, we had an agreement to do it that way God Almighty grant our wish. So, I wish you let us join hands together and wed us together.

Mr. Gilbert: Fine! Nice idea. I am in support.

Mrs. Gilbert: me too.

Lauren: Thank you ma'am and sir! Katherine! (she hugged her).

Katherine: Am so happy uhm! You find your partner and he didn't betray your trust. Am happy and joyful may he be yours forever.

Lauren: Thanks.... uhm (they laughed).

****

ACT THIRTEEN

(WEDDING DAY)

(it's *Katherine and Lauren wedding, the two friends were happy, the wedding gown they were both wearing is an exclusive, the facial make up gave them both a major transformation, if it's worn on a normal day, no one could recognize them. Dylan and Irene also had beautiful same gown.)*

(Jacob mummy's condition is very different, she was present also, Barros is looking amazing in Black suit that speaks for him that he is the new CEO of Abakad pharmacy.)

(the couples set to come out on the stage)

M.C: Chim, chim, chim, ah, ah (preparing his speech) hello, we gathered here for Katherine and Lauren's wedding and the grooms are Jacob and Daniel.

Crowd: (applaud).

M.C: Ma'am (facing Jacob's mother and families) what did you have to say to the couples?

Mrs. James: I hope they understand each other and bound for freedom!

M.C: Sir (facing Jacob) your turn.

Jacob: I promised to be hers' forever and wish we are happily married.

M.C: Sir (Katherine's dad)

Mr. Gilbert: I wish for their union, Katherine and Lauren are best friends, I wish their grooms co-operate with each other too and form two family and forever in love.

Crowd: (applaud).

M.C: Ma'am (Katherine's mother).

Mrs. Gilbert: Same here!

Crowd: WOW! (cheers).

Lauren: I'm in love with you and am yours forever, no one shall separate us.

Jacob: I promise to be yours forever too, I love you. (hugged and kisses flying)

Katherine: (he turned to Daniel) finally, I am yours, I will forever love you.

Daniel: i love you more babe. (he hugged and kiss her)

Daniel Dad: that's my son, I am proud of him. (telling Kate) I love you son (he shouted)

MC: let the party begin. Dj, play the music let's have fun.

Crowd: yeeeaaaaa.

THE END

****

ACKNOWLEDGEMENT

All praise belongs to Almighty God, Gratitude to him for sparing my life and letting this book to see the light of the day. I once again thank him for blessing me with the knowledge to pen down this book.

Ample adoration to late Mr. Amusan Abdullateef And Mrs. Amusan Bolatito (My Parents). May their soul rest in perfect peace.

The fruition of this Art work would have been impossible to achieve without the constant motivation from my Remarkable sponsor jimoh Sulyman.

I also want to thank Alhaja Shakiroh Aduke Elelu, Alhaja Kamaldeen Muslimah, Alhaja Amuda Kanike Aminah, Alhaji Kamaldeen Al-Ameen and Families.

The luxurious support received from Yusuf Asiata Ajoke and Muhammed Akanbi Shittu is immeasurable.

About The Author

AMUSAN AISHAT ABIODUN Amusan Aishat Abiodun is a native of Ilorin west Local Government, Kwara state, Nigeria. She Birthed her PSCL (primary school leaving certificate) and SSCE/WAEC (secondary school certificate) at kwara state Model Secondary School, she also Bagged her NCE (Nigeria certificate of Education) at kwara state college of Education, Ilorin, Kwara state, Nigeria. Her Bachelor Degree was secured at university of Ilorin, Nigeria.

She is a socialist and explorer. Aishat engages in marketing, Fabrics designs and writing.

She is as well a publisher of two books and voluminous poems.

Untitled

This page was intentionally left to be blank for Note Taking.

www.ingramcontent.com/pod-product-compliance
Lightning Source LLC
LaVergne TN
LVHW052058160826
845678LV00015B/3280

* 9 7 9 8 3 5 2 3 7 6 1 7 1 *